UNICORN

IS MAYBE NOT SO GREAT AFTER ALL

Bob Shea

Disney•HYPERION/Los Angeles   New York

For information address Disney • Hyperion,
125 West End Avenue, New York, New York 10023.

First Hardcover Edition, July 2019
1 3 5 7 9 10 8 6 4 2
FAC-029191-19144
Printed in Malaysia

Library of Congress Cataloging-in-Publication Data

Names: Shea, Bob, author, illustrator.
Title: Unicorn is maybe not so great after all / Bob Shea.
Description: First edition. Los Angeles ; New York :
Disney-Hyperion, 2019.
Summary: Concerned about losing friends during the
first week of school, Unicorn upgrades his fabulousness.
Identifiers: LCCN 2018009068 ISBN 9781368009447
Subjects: CYAC: Unicorns—Fiction. First day of school—Fiction.
Friendship—Fiction.
Classification: LCC PZ7.S53743 UI 2019   DDC [E]—dc23
LC record available at https://lccn.loc.gov/2018009068

Reinforced binding

Visit www.DisneyBooks.com

It's finally here! The first day of school!

Have a great day!

BALD →
EAGLE

Every day is great when you're a
super-special unicorn!

CONTRACTUALLY OBLIGATED FIRST-DAY JITTERS

BUTTER

Ugh, first day of school.

My stomach is full of butterflies.
And not just because I ate all
those butterflies.

Don't be silly!

There's nothing to be nervous about! But let me go first, in case there are photographers.

Being a unicorn used to mean something around here.

But now all anyone cares about are rubber bands that look like other things.

HEY UNICORN,
WHY THE LONG FACE?

Goat, do people say I'm a yawn-icorn?

What? No! No one says anything about you at all.

But everyone is sure bananas for these fantastic new rubber bands that look like all sorts of different things!

I love school.

New and fantastic, eh?

That's it! I'll be the n e w e s t, most fantastic unicorn this school—nay, the world—has ever seen.

Thanks Goat, you're a true friend.

A SOCCER BALL!

My plan is so simple, so perfect.

RAINBOW WIG

HORN ENHANCER

TAIL EXTENSION

BIG FAKE TEETH

TEMPORARY TATTOO

COLORED CONTACT LENSES

SASSY SATIN SHORTS

GO-GO BOOTS

NEW-NICORN	#87

- SASS
- RAZZLE
- DAZZLE
- WHIMSY
- MAGIC
- JE NE SAIS QUOI

They'll forget all about their silly
rubber bands once they get a load
of my sassy new look and cheery,
whimsical attitude.

Hey Unicorn, what's with the . . .

Sparkles and whimsy!

Ahh! It got in my mouth!
What the hey!

Looks like people are too starstruck to sit near the razzle-dazzle and sparkle-barkle of a shiny new-nicorn.

Can ya blame 'em?

With my horn in the way,
I can't help the school win on
the soccer field, but I can wow 'em
with a crowd-pleasing halftime
showstopper.

Please don't . . .

Wheeeee!

Making it rain cupcakes is so yesterday.
Get a load of these full-size, flaming birthday cakes!

Go, team!

GO HOME, UNICORN!

Sob!

I've ruined everything.

A stale bran mini-muffin? Great. Now I have no friends *and* no magic.

Where have you been,
Unicorn? We missed
you at school today.

Whoa!

Somebody crack a window.
Just look at this mess!
Did a clown explode in here?

SNACKS

BOARD
GAMES

But . . . I thought you guys were mad at me?

You've been super-annoying, for sure, but you're still our friend.

You feeling okay, Unicorn?
Are you going to puke or
something?

No. Actually,
I'm feeling kinda . . .

A BASEBALL

A PEA

A FANCY
GOLD RING

A MANHOLE
COVER

A BLOWHOLE

A BALL
BEARING

AN ORANGE

A GOLD
DOUBLOON

A RUBBER
BAND

THE SUN

A ROUND
THING

A MARBLE